What's Michael?

Sleepless Nights

Story and Art:
Makoto Kobayashi

Translation:
**Dana Lewis, Lea Hernandez,
& Toren Smith**

Dark Horse Manga™

Lettering and Retouch:
Sno Cone Studios

publisher
Mike Richardson

series editor
Philip Simon

series executive editor
Toren Smith for **Studio Proteus**

collection editor
Chris Warner

designer
Mark Cox and Heidi Fainza

art director
Lia Ribacchi

English-language version produced by
Studio Proteus and **Dark Horse Comics, Inc.**

What's Michael? Vol. X: Sleepless Nights

This volume collects **What's Michael?** stories
from issues thirty-nine through forty-eight
of the Dark Horse comic-book series **Super
Manga Blast**!

The artwork of this volume has been produced as
a mirror-image of the original Japanese edition to
conform to English-language standards.

Published by
Dark Horse Manga
A division of Dark Horse Comics, Inc.
10956 SE Main Street
Milwaukie, OR 97222

darkhorse.com

To find a comics shop in your area, call the
Comic Shop Locator Service toll-free at
1-888-266-4226

First edition: June 2005
ISBN: 1-59307-337-2

10 9 8 7 6 5 4 3 2 1

Printed in the U.S.A.

POPO'S SLEEPING HABITS

ONCE UPON
A TIME, A COUPLE
NAMED MICHAEL
AND POPO LIVED
HAPPILY
TOGETHER.

WHENEVER MICHAEL SLEPT ON THE TELEVISION...

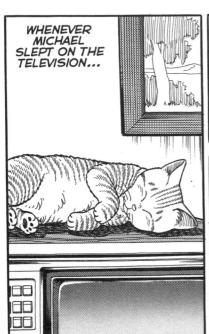

...SWEET LITTLE POPO WOULD CURL UP BESIDE HIM.

ONLY, POPO HAD *AWFUL* SLEEPING HABITS, SO...

...SHE'D *PUSH* AND *PUSH* HER DEAR MICHAEL UNTIL...

...HE FELL OFF.

YOWR!

4

NOTICING WHAT SHE'D DONE...

...POPO WOULD RUN AFTER MICHAEL TO APOLOGIZE.

ONLY...

MRR ...?

.....?

.....!

!?!

5

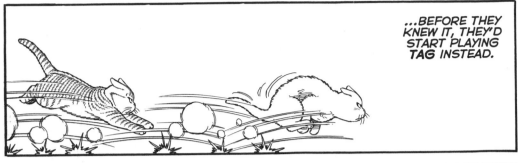

...BEFORE THEY KNEW IT, THEY'D START PLAYING **TAG** INSTEAD.

MRR...?

SOMETIMES MICHAEL WOULD THINK...

..."POPO'S SO ADORABLE WHEN SHE'S SLEEPING."

AND SUDDENLY HE'D FEEL LIKE TELLING HER HOW MUCH HE LOVED HER.

FAP

NNN... MROW...?

.....
.....

ONLY...

..."A CAT'S MEMORY LASTS THREE STEPS," THE SAYING GOES.

SO HE'D ALWAYS FORGET WHY HE'D COME OVER.

.....:
.....?

AND HE'D GET SO FRUSTRATED HE'D BITE HER INSTEAD.

CHOMP

FROWR!

FSST!
NYOW!

FROWWL!!!

SO THEY'D HAVE ANOTHER "LOVER'S QUARREL."

THEY DID LOVE EACH OTHER VERY MUCH, MICHAEL AND POPO...

...STILL, SOMETIMES MICHAEL WOULD WANT TO SLEEP ALONE.

SO HE'D GO HIDE ON TOP OF THE CLOTHES CABINET.

7

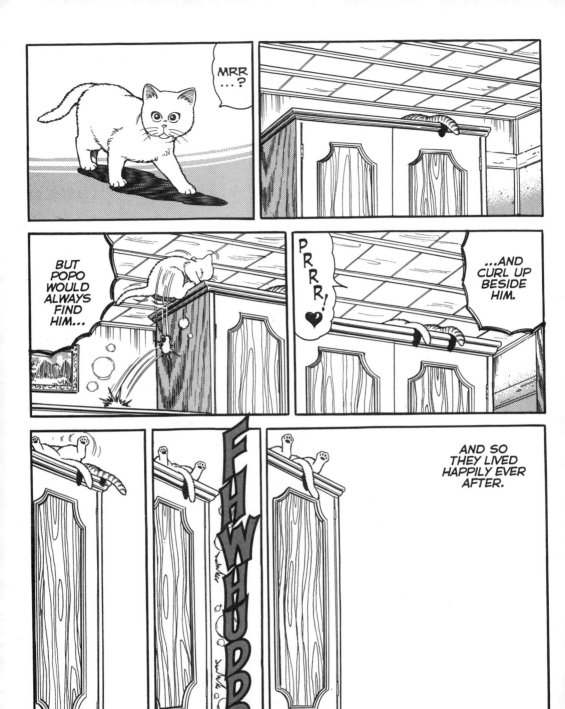

THE END

....
....

THE BOTTOM LINE IS...

...IT DOESN'T SELL.

WE'VE RUN COMMERCIALS, CUT OUR PRICES, OFFERED PRIZES...

WHY WON'T IT SELL?!

UH... SIR?

MAYBE...

MAYBE BECAUSE IT TASTES BAD...?

WHA--?!

ARE YOU SERIOUS?!

LET ME DEMONSTRATE, SIR. WE HAVE HERE A CAT THAT HASN'T EATEN FOR *THREE DAYS*.

YOWWR! NYOWW!

AND *THIS*...

...IS A FRESHLY OPENED TIN OF *MORNING KAT*.

HERE, MICHAEL! *DIN-DIN!* HERE, KITTY, KITTY!

MROWR! ♥

!

....
...?

COME ON! DON'T BE SHY! EAT UP!

HERE!! HELP *YOUR-SELF!*

YOWR....! ♥

PRRR...! PRRR...!! ♥

SLRP
MNCH
GLP

HA HA HA! YOU DON'T HAVE TO RUSH...TAKE YOUR TIME!

...! ...! ...!

WHAT IS SO BAD ABOUT *MORNING KAT?*

ONLY *FELINES* KNOW FOR SURE.

BUT THE *BATTLE* FOR THE *JAPANESE CAT FOOD MARKET* HAS JUST BEGUN! *FIGHT ON,* MORNING KAT INCORPORATED!!

THE END

16

17

HRM ...?

DARN IT, POPO!

YOU *KNOW* YOU'RE *FORBIDDEN* TO GROOM DURING CLASS!

SUS-PENDED!

MROWR ?!

RRR ...!

....!

HEY, YOU! *REX!*

PERMED HAIR VIOLATES THE DRESS CODE!

SUS-PENDED!

VRMBBBB

**THINGS THAT
GO DUMP
IN THE NIGHT**

HEH
HEH
HEH...

BABES
GALORE...!

*THE
COUNT!
DREAD
VAMPIRE!*

21

AND THE MOST DANGEROUS VAMPIRE OF THEM ALL...FOR HE FEARS NOT THE DAYLIGHT SUN!

AND *NOW*, TO FEED HIS LUST FOR THE *FRESH BLOOD* OF *NUBILE YOUNG WOMEN*, HE'S SOLD THE *FAMILY ESTATE* IN *TRANSYLVANIA*, BOUGHT A *BABEMOBILE*, AND MOTORED INTO *TOWN!!*

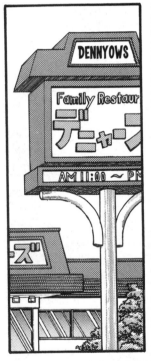

DENNYOWS

Family Restaur

AM 11:00 ~ PM

--AND THERE WAS *GOUTS* OF *BLOOD* SPRAYED ACROSS THE *WINDOW!!*

E E K!

THAT'S SO *HORRIBLE!*

HEY, HEY, *CHICKIES!*

WHAT'S A BUNCH OF NICE GIRLS LIKE YOU DOING IN A PLACE LIKE THIS?

HUH ...?

OH, WE'RE TELLING *HORROR STORIES!*

LIKE, Y'KNOW-- "WHICH ONE'S *SCARIEST?*"

OH, YEAH ...?

THEN LET *ME* SIT IN, GALS!!

THEY CALL ME THE *KING* OF *HORROR*!

REALLY?! AWESOME!

HEH HEH HEH...

SEEING AS I'M THE *REAL* THING...!

OKAY... MY TURN!

THIS HAPPENED ON THAT LITTLE ROAD SOUTH OUT OF TOWN...

...AND *EVERY* *WORD* IS *TRUE*!

"LATE ONE NIGHT, THIS HIGH SCHOOL GYM TEACHER WAS TAKING THAT ROAD HOME.

BRAPPPP

"HE CAME AROUND A CURVE, AND... THERE WAS A *CAT* SMACK IN THE *MIDDLE OF THE ROAD*!"

OH *NO!!*

S
K
R
E
E
E

"HE SLAMMED ON HIS BRAKES, BUT IT WAS *TOO LATE!*"

"CERTAIN HE'D HIT THE POOR CREATURE, HE STOPPED...

"...THEN GOT OUT AND LOOKED TO SEE IF IT WAS OKAY, BUT...*NO CAT ANYWHERE!*"

HUH ...!

JUST *SEEIN'* THINGS ...?

"SO THE TEACHER GOT BACK IN HIS CAR AND DROVE ON.

BRAPPPP

"THEN HE GLANCED INTO HIS REAR-VIEW MIRROR, AND--"

HNN ...?

WAUGH!!

THERE WAS AN *ANGRY CAT* GLARING AT HIM!

....?!

.....

"HE SLAMMED ON THE BRAKES AND LOOKED BACK...

"...BUT THERE WAS *NO CAT THERE!*"

B-BUT THEN...

HE LOOKED *CLOSER,* AND...

....?!

AH ...?!

25

THE END

BEAT THE HEAT

27

28

WHEN I TOOK THEM IN FOR THEIR *SHOTS*, THE *VET* SAID...

...IT'S GOING TO BE A *HOT* SUMMER.

SHALL I GIVE THEM A *TRIM*?

AND SO I, I...

BUT I NEVER *DREAMED* SHE'D BE SO *DEPRESSED!!*

WHAT DID YOU *EXPECT*?!

MICHAEL AND *MINI-MICHAEL* ARE BAD ENOUGH, BUT *POPO'S* A GIRL!

HER *FUR* IS HER *LIFE!*

I'M *SORRY*, POPO!

IT'LL GROW BACK IN *NO TIME!*

SO CHEER UP, OKAY?

NYOWR! RRR!!

OH, NO! POPO!!

FWHDD

29

DO SOME-THING!

SHE'LL BE SCARRED FOR LIFE!!

...

OH! OH, YES...

...THAT JUST MIGHT WORK...

SQUEE

FWHSSH

HUH.

32

THE END

MELANCHOLY ALYCE

≈SIGH≈

NURSE. IS MAH ALYCE STILL GRIEVIN'?

YES, SUH.

MISS ALYCE AIN'T EATEN PROP'LY FOR *THREE* DAYS.

THA'S *ENOUGH.*

ALYCE, LOVE...

...PULL YUHSELF T'GETHER, DAUGHTER.

T'WAS JUST A *GOLDFISH.*

WILL YOU NEVAH UNDERSTAN' TH' *DEPTHS* OF MAH *FEELIN'S*, PAPAW?!

GOLDY GOLDFISH WAS MAH *BOSOM COMPANION!* MAH O-ONLIEST *FRIEN'!*

OH, *GOLDYYY!*

B_AWWW!

OH, ALYCE...

TWO DAYS SPED BY...

34

ALYCE!

ALYCE, LOVE! WHERE ARE YOU?

HERE, PAPA.

ALYCE!

AH BRUNG YOU A *PRESENT*, MAH DEAR!

A *PRESENT?* AH DON'T--

NOW, DARLIN'... JUST *OPEN* IT.

AH *PROMISE* YOU'LL *LIKE* IT!

O-OKAY.

OH!!

MEWW!

35

OH, *PAPAW!* HE'S THE CUTEST THANG *EVAH!*

HAH HAH! AH *KNEW* YOU'D LIKE HIM!

NOW, DAUGHTER, LET GOLDY *REST IN PEACE...*

...AN' YOU BE YOUR SWEET, HAPPY SELF AGAIN!

YES, PAPAW!

THANK YOU!

AND SO...

PAPAW! GUESS *WHAT?!*

WHAT, ALYCE?

MAH LITTLE *MICHAEL?*

WHEN HE'S ALL *HAPPY...*HE *PURRS!*

HA HA !!!

WHAT A *SCAMP!*

36

PAPAW! PAPAW, OH MAH GOSH!

LITTLE MICHAEL?

HE *WASHES* HIS *FACE!* LIKE *THIS!*

HA HA HA! IS THAT SO?

MISS ALYCE HAS BEEN RIGHT *CHEERFUL* SINCE MICHAEL CAME.

MICHAEL HAS GIVEN US BACK OUR SWEET ALYCE!

PAPAW! PAPAW! *LISSEN!*

HA HA! WHAT ABOUT MICHAEL NOW?

TP TP TP

NOT *MICHAEL! ME!*

AH KILLED A *FLY!*

AH LEARNED HOW FROM *MICHAEL!*

AH CAN KILL *FLIES* AN' *ROACHES* AND *EVERYTHIN'!*

THAS'... NICE...

THE END

SLEEPLESS NIGHTS

NO...

...GOOD.

YAWW

MAYBE A DIFFERENT SPOT...?

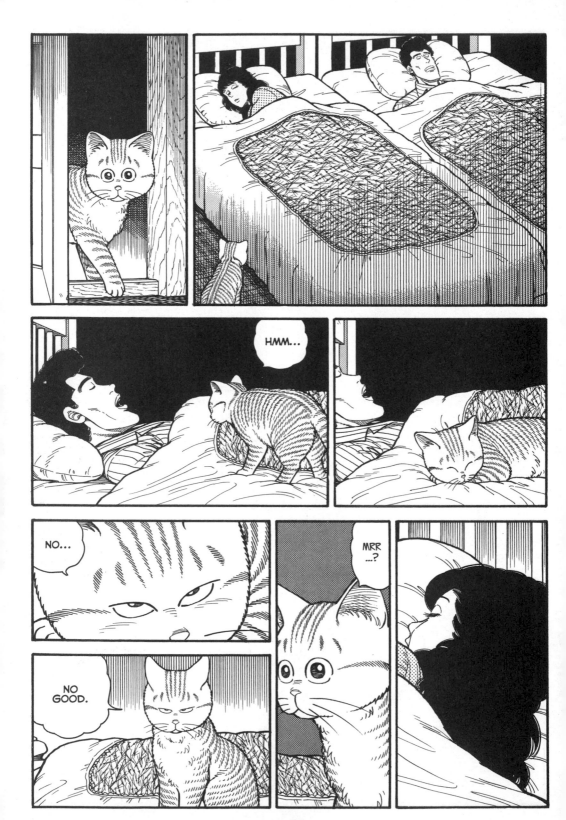

40

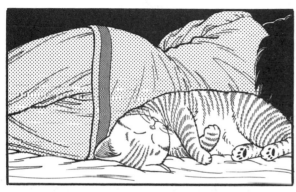

NO.

NO GOOD.

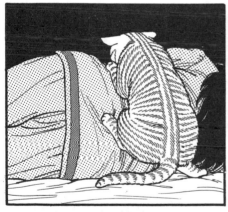
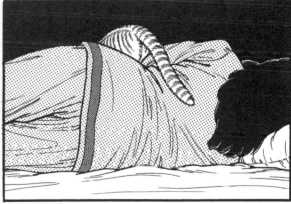

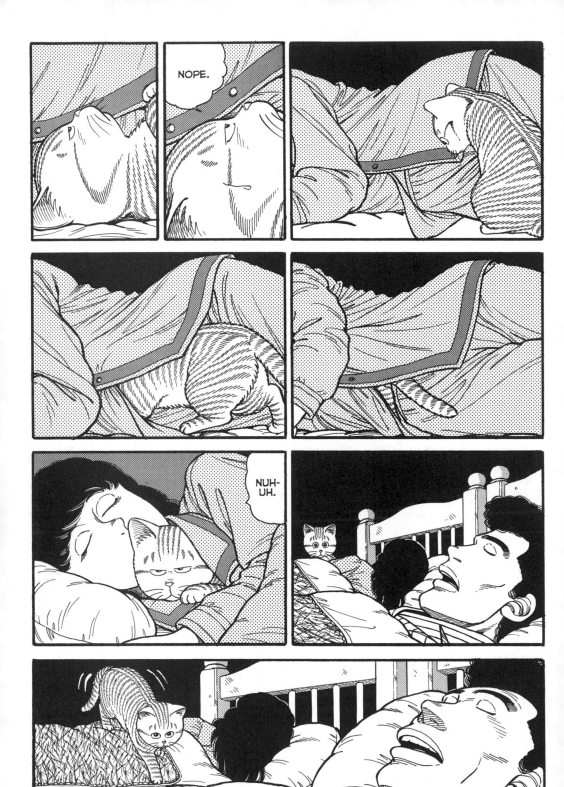

THE END

THE BOSS'S LAMENT

IT'S BOSS CHARLES!!

GOOD MORNING, BOSS!!

GOOD MORNING!

HRMM...

MIKE!

BOSS!!

CUTE APRON, KID.

AW, GEEZ...

HEE HYA HYA HYA HYA!!

HMM ...?

'MORNING, SIR.

YO, LADY. GOOD NEWS, I SEE?

WHEN'S THE BIG DAY?

NEXT MONTH, AROUND THE *TENTH.*

I *SEE.*

EAT WELL, AND TAKE *CARE* OF YOURELF.

A BOSS MUST BE **STRONG**, BUT **KIND**. A BOSS MUST EARN THE **ABSOLUTE TRUST** OF HIS CATS.

BOSS CHARLES. A BOSS AMONG BOSSES!

WE'LL, I'VE CHECKED OUT THE TURF.

NOW TO CATCH A **CATNAP**...

HEY, CAT!

NO **DOZIN'** ON THE **STAIRS!** MOVE IT!

B T U M P P

FUGYAH!

....
....

SKRTCH
SKRTCH
SKRTCH

49

THE END

CHARUMERA TAKAHASHI. NICKNAME: CHARLES!

BOSS OF A VAST TURF, RUNNING FROM WARD ONE TO WARD FOUR.

HEIR TO THE THRONE

THE WORLD OF CATS IS A CLASS SOCIETY. AND CHARLES STANDS AT THE VERY PEAK.

HELLO, BOSS!!

G'DAY, BOSS CHARLES!

HRMF...

TOURED THE 'HOOD. ALL'S GOOD...

THINK I'LL SPEND THE NIGHT AT SANDRA'S...

51

HHN... I CAN'T GO EMPTY-HANDED.

....
....

FRESH FISH!! STEP RIGHT UP!!

LONG LIFE FISH

HEY, YA DANG MANGE BALL!! THIEF!!

FISH

YO!! SANDRA!!

CHARLES!!

52

JIRO'S HARD WORKING, BUT HE'S GOT *CATNIP* ON HIS BACK.

IF *THEY* CAN'T...

NO... CATZILLA'S A *DAME*. RULES DON'T *ALLOW* IT.

WHICH MEANS...

AGE-WISE...

MICHAEL'S ALL WE GOT...

EH ...?!

YOU *MEAN* IT?!

M- M- ME?!

THE NEXT *BOSS*?!

THAT'S RIGHT.

HNG ...?

AH?!

BOSS CHARLES!!

WELCOME HOME.

YO. HOW'VE YOU BEEN? COME OUTTA THAT HOLE SO I CAN SEE YOU.

UH... GEE...

ACT-UALLY...

THE NEIGHBOR CATS MUSCLED IN...

...AND THIS IS ALL WE GOT LEFT!

WHA ...?!

MICHAEL!! WHAT WERE YOU DOING?!

BOSS CHARLES. HE WON'T BE RETIRING ANYTIME SOON...

THE END

DROWNING IN LOVE

POP...

FWAP

MRRT!

CHOMPF

TPP TPP TPP TPP

HUH?

...!

TMP TPP TPP TPP

I'LL BE...!

SKRK

FLAP FLAP
FLAP

DOONK

KRASSSH

FLAP FLAP FLAP

CRAZY BIRD.

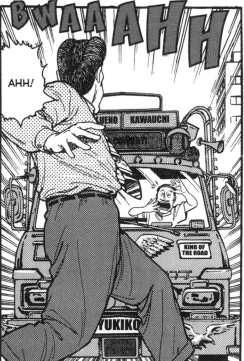

BWAAAAHH

AHH!

UENO KAWAUCHI

KING OF THE ROAD

YUKIKO

NOOO!

GROWF!

RMMMBL

SLRP

≷HAFF≷
≷HANF≷

FWMP

HEY, PUNK!

YOU KNOW WHO YOU'RE MESSIN' WITH?!

I-I'M!!

AIIEEE!

UH... OKAY...

THE END

HRFF HRFF HRFF HRFF!

AH HA HA HA! COME *BACK HERE*, BEAR!

AH!

BOW-WOW!

BOW-WOW!!

BOW-WOW!!

THAT'S *RIGHT!*

SEE THE BIG *BOW-WOW!*

AMAZING, TAMAMI!

YOU KNOW "*BOW-WOW*" ...!

MY *LITTLE GENIUS!*

BOW-WOW!! BOW-WOW!!

WHAT'S THAT *OVER THERE*, TAMAMI?

....
....

MOW-
MOW!

MOW-
MOW!!

MOW-
MOW!!

NOT
"MOW-MOW,"
TAMAMI. IT'S
*"MEOW-
MEOW."*

AH HA HA!
BUT GOOD
ENOUGH
FOR
NEEOW!

Z
W
E
E
E
E
E
E
OOWEEE
OOWEEE

HEY!

HEAR
THE
CICA-
DAS?!

*READY,
TAMAMI?*

THIS TIME,
LET'S DO
CICADAS.

ZWEEEE
ZWEE
ZWEE
ZWEE!!

ZUH-WEEEE
ZWEE ZWEE
ZWEE!!

65

YOUR TURN, BABY!!

....
....

MOWWW MOW MOW MOW!!

MOWWW MOW MOW MOW!!

LITTLE TAMAMI WAS BEGINNING TO TALK.

OKAY! THIS TIME SAY "SHAYYY"...

SHAYYY!!

TRY IT!

MOWWW!!

WHAT... ARE YOU... TEACHING HER?!

TAMAMI LOVED PLAYING WITH MINI-MICHAEL...

AH! AH! AHH!!

FWOMMP

NEOWRR!

OH, BAD GIRL!

MINI-MICHAEL OUCHY-OUCHIES!

...ESPECIALLY SINCE HE WAS SO FAT AND SQUISHY.

MEANWHILE, MICHAEL AND POPO HAD THEIR SECOND LITTER OF KITTENS...

...EENY-MICHAEL...

...MEENY-MICHAEL...

...MINEY-MICHAEL...

...AND THEIR LONG-AWAITED BABY GIRL.

RA!

HUNGRY! I'M HUNGRY!!

FTAMM
FTAM

I'LL NURSE YOU IN A MINUTE!

MOMMA! POOPY!!

HOLD ON!

EENY-MICHAEL! GET OUT OF THERE!

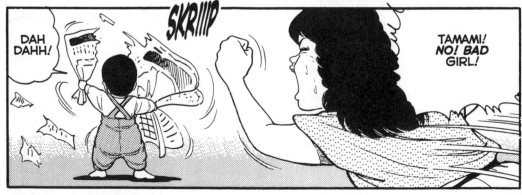

DAH DAHH!

SKRIIIP

TAMAMI! NO! BAD GIRL!

68

OOOH!!

YOU MEN!! STOP *GOOFING OFF* AND *HELP US!!*

IT WAS A HARD TIME FOR THE LADIES.

YO.

MIKE. POPO.

BOSS!

BOSS *CHARLES* ...!

CON- GRATS, KIDS.

BRING 'EM UP *STRONG.*

THANK YOU, SIR. WE *WILL,* SIR.

YOU'RE TOO KIND, SIR.

MICHAEL, YOU'RE A LUCKY CAT...

HN??

WHY'S THAT, DAISUKE...?

YOUR WIFE... SUCH A *BEAUTY*...

WHATCHA DOIN'??

GET YOUR *TAIL* IN GEAR!!

YES, DEAR!

....
....

....
....

DAHH!

DAHH!

UNG
...

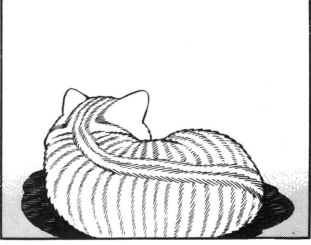

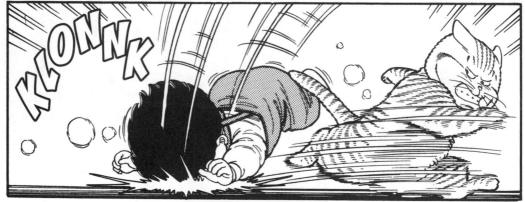

72

MICHAEL AND POPO'S KITTENS GROW BIGGER *BY THE DAY...*

BIGGER AND BIGGER!

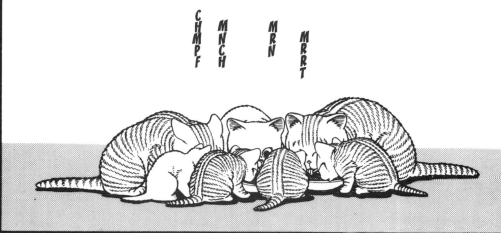

MN?

....?

MICHAEL! POPO! MINI-MIKE! EENY-MIKE! MEENY-MIKE! MINEY-MIKE! RA!

SUPPER TIME! ♥

MREE-OWW! ♥

THD THD THDD THDTHD

RA?

RAAA! HERE, KITTY KITTY KITTY!

IT'S YOUR FAVORITE!

♥

MEW-ROW!

TMP

SPLAT

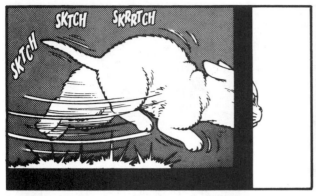

THE END

AOWNN!

....
....

FSSSK!

WHLAM!

STOP THAT *YOWLING!* I *FED* YOU ALREADY!

WHY WON'T YOU *EAT* IT?!

MORNING CAT

THIS IS THE *FINEST STUFF* WE MAKE!

NOW, EAT IT!!

YAWW!

NOWW!

NOWN!

SKRTCH

SKRTCH

NOWN!

FINE. I *GET* IT. YOU DON'T LIKE OUR CAT FOOD.

THE END